KEVIN HENKES

OWEN'S MARSHMALLOW CHICK

A Greenwillow Book
HarperFestival®
A Division of HarperCollinsPublishers

On Easter morning, Owen's basket was full.

In it were jelly beans

and gumdrops

and buttercream eggs

and a big chocolate bunny

and a little marshmallow chick.

Owen looked at the jelly beans.

"My favorite," he said.

And he ate them up.

Owen looked at the gumdrops.

"My favorite," he said.

And he ate them up.

Owen looked at the buttercream eggs.

"My favorite," he said.

And he ate them up.

Owen looked at the chocolate bunny.

"My favorite," he said.

And he ate it up.

Owen looked at the marshmallow chick.

It was the same color

as his fuzzy yellow blanket.

Owen played with his chick all morning.

Owen played with his chick all afternoon.

At bedtime, Owen put the chick

on his shelf with his best toys.

"My favorite," he said.

And he kissed it good-night.